MW01493781

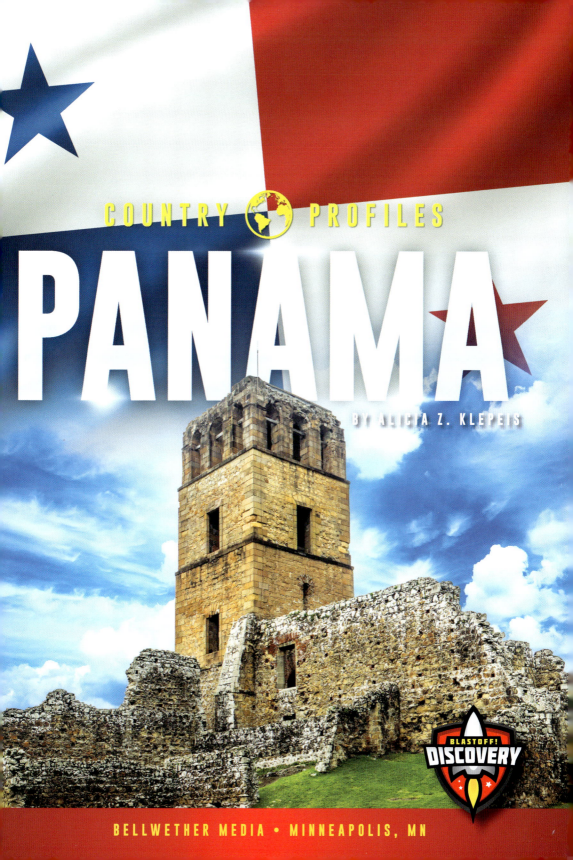

COUNTRY 🌎 PROFILES

PANAMA

BY ALICIA Z. KLEPEIS

BLASTOFF!
DISCOVERY

BELLWETHER MEDIA • MINNEAPOLIS, MN

Blastoff! Discovery launches a new mission: reading to learn. Filled with facts and features, each book offers you an exciting new world to explore!

BLASTOFF! UNIVERSE

BLASTOFF! Beginners — GRADE K

BLASTOFF! READERS — GRADES 1-3

BLASTOFF! DISCOVERY — GRADE 4

This edition first published in 2023 by Bellwether Media, Inc.

No part of this publication may be reproduced in whole or in part without written permission of the publisher.
For information regarding permission, write to Bellwether Media, Inc.,
Attention: Permissions Department,
6012 Blue Circle Drive, Minnetonka, MN 55343.

Library of Congress Cataloging-in-Publication Data

Names: Klepeis, Alicia, 1971- author.
Title: Panama / by Alicia Z. Klepeis.
Description: Minneapolis : Bellwether Media, 2023. | Series: Country
    profiles | Includes bibliographical references and index. |
    Audience: Ages 7-13 | Audience: Grades 4-6 | Summary:
    "Engaging images accompany information about Panama.
    The combination of high-interest subject matter and narrative text is
    intended for students in grades 3 through 8"–Provided by publisher.
Identifiers: LCCN 2022016491 (print) | LCCN 2022016492 (ebook)
    | ISBN 9781644877487 (library binding) | ISBN
    9781648347948 (ebook)
Subjects: LCSH: Panama–Juvenile literature.
Classification: LCC F1563.2 .K54 2023 (print) | LCC F1563.2
    (ebook) | DDC 972.87–dc23/eng/20220414
LC record available at https://lccn.loc.gov/2022016491
LC ebook record available at https://lccn.loc.gov/2022016492

Editor: Rebecca Sabelko   Designer: Brittany McIntosh

Printed in the United States of America, North Mankato, MN.

TABLE OF CONTENTS

A group of **tourists** boards a boat in Santa Catalina on Panama's Pacific coast. The ocean breeze sweeps across the deck of the boat. Suddenly, a humpback whale slaps its huge tail against the ocean's surface. Splash!

OTHER TOP SITES

BARÚ VOLCANO NATIONAL PARK

BIOMUSEO

DARIÉN NATIONAL PARK

PANAMA CANAL

The group arrives at Coiba Island. It is 1 of 38 islands in Coiba National Park. Some people **snorkel** just off the white sand beach. Fish of every color dart past in the bright blue water. Other people hike through the **rain forest** on a trail. Howler monkeys call to each other in the trees. A scarlet macaw flies overhead. Welcome to Panama!

COSTA RICA

DAVID

PANAMA

SANTIAGO

PACIFIC OCEAN

N
W + E
S

Panama is a country in Central America. It covers an area of 29,120 square miles (75,420 square kilometers). The nation's capital is Panama City. It stands in east-central Panama, close to the Panama **Canal**. This important waterway is about 40 miles (64 kilometers) long. It connects the Pacific and Atlantic Oceans.

Panama is an **isthmus** that links North America and South America. The waters of the Caribbean Sea wash onto its northern shores. Colombia is Panama's eastern neighbor. The Pacific Ocean crashes on the southern coast. The nation of Costa Rica borders Panama to the west.

LANDSCAPE AND CLIMATE

Mountains run through the center of Panama. The Panama Canal passes between the two main ranges. The highest peaks, including a **volcano** called Barú, stand in the west. The land gradually slopes downward into lowlands along both coasts. Many rivers start in the mountains. The Indio flows into the Caribbean Sea. The Chepo drains into the Pacific Ocean.

BARÚ VOLCANO

INDIO RIVER

CHEPO RIVER

N W E S

BARÚ VOLCANO

PANAMA CITY

Average seasonal highs and lows

JANUARY
HIGH: 88 °F (31 °C)
LOW: 73 °F (23 °C)

APRIL
HIGH: 90 °F (32 °C)
LOW: 75 °F (24 °C)

JULY
HIGH: 86 °F (30 °C)
LOW: 75 °F (24 °C)

OCTOBER
HIGH: 84 °F (29 °C)
LOW: 73 °F (23 °C)

°F = degrees Fahrenheit
°C = degrees Celsius

INCREDIBLE ISLANDS

Over 1,600 islands lie off Panama's coasts. People from around the world travel to these islands to surf and scuba dive.

Panama has a **tropical** climate affected by the central mountains. The Caribbean side of the country receives rain year-round. The Pacific side experiences a dry season from January to April.

Despite its small size, Panama is home to many amazing animals. Dolphins dive and whales make giant splashes in the waters off the coasts. Several species of sea turtles lay their eggs on Panama's coastal beaches.

Large rodents called agoutis search the rain forest for nuts and fruits. Overhead, toucans bark and growl at each other from their perches in the trees. Spider monkeys swing quickly from one branch to the next. Colorful poison frogs hop about and eat insects. The strawberry poison frog can vary between blue and red, depending on where it lives in Panama.

KEEL-BILLED TOUCAN

AGOUTI

GREEN SEA TURTLE

OCELOT

MANY BIG CATS

Several kinds of big cats dwell in Barú Volcano National Park. Jaguars and pumas are the largest. Ocelots, jaguarundis, and margays prowl in the park, too.

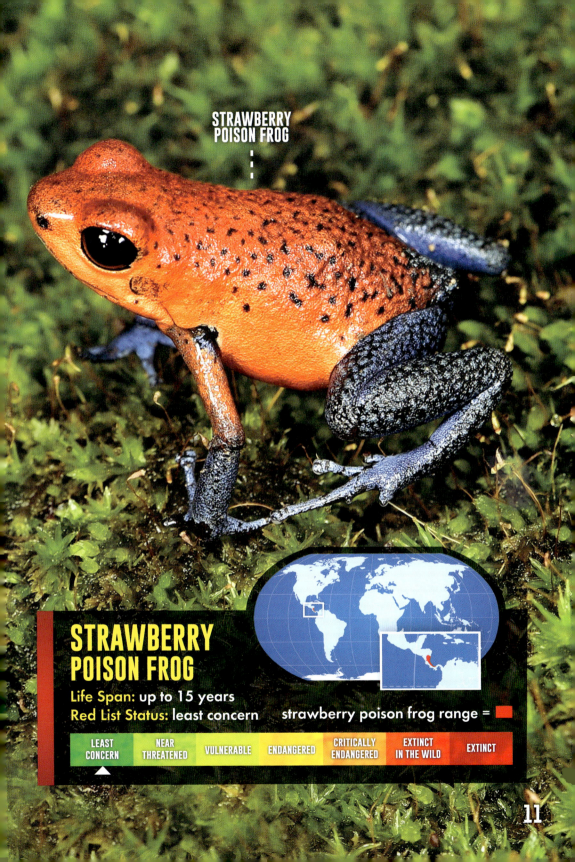

STRAWBERRY
POISON FROG

STRAWBERRY POISON FROG

Life Span: up to 15 years
Red List Status: least concern

strawberry poison frog range = 🟥

LEAST CONCERN	NEAR THREATENED	VULNERABLE	ENDANGERED	CRITICALLY ENDANGERED	EXTINCT IN THE WILD	EXTINCT

Panama is home to more than 4 million people. Roughly 2 out of 3 are *mestizos*. They have **Indigenous** and European **ancestors**. Many Native American groups continue to call Panama home. The largest include the Ngäbe and Kuna. Nearly 1 in 10 people are Black or have African ancestors. People throughout Latin America, the United States, and China **immigrate** to Panama seeking jobs.

Almost half of Panamanians are Roman Catholic. Other forms of Christianity are also commonly practiced. Spanish is the official language of Panama. But many people are **bilingual**. They speak an Indigenous language or English as well as Spanish.

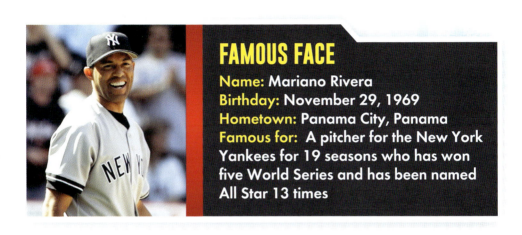

FAMOUS FACE

Name: Mariano Rivera
Birthday: November 29, 1969
Hometown: Panama City, Panama
Famous for: A pitcher for the New York Yankees for 19 seasons who has won five World Series and has been named All Star 13 times

SPEAK SPANISH

ENGLISH	SPANISH	HOW TO SAY IT
hello	hola	OH-la
goodbye	adiós	ah-dee-OHS
please	por favor	pohr fah-VOR
thank you	gracias	grah-SEE-ahs
yes	sí	SEE
no	no	noh

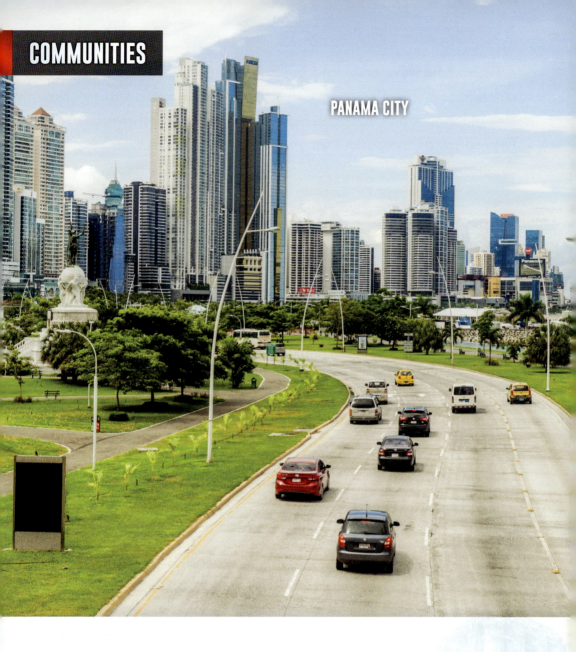

PANAMA CITY

Nearly 7 out of 10 Panamanians live in **urban** areas. About 1.9 million people dwell in the nation's biggest city, Panama City. Most live in houses made of cement. However, apartments are growing more popular. People often travel by buses and cars. A metro system opened in the capital in 2014.

Families in the countryside usually live in houses. The Emberá and the Ngäbe-Buglé live in homes on stilts. This protects their homes from flooding. People in **rural** areas often walk or take buses to get around.

COLÓN ISLAND

AN ECO-VILLAGE

One town on Panama's Colón Island is the world's first plastic bottle village. The homes are built from wire cages filled with plastic bottles. Just one home may use 20,000 bottles!

15

People in Panama enjoy a wide variety of music. Popular styles include salsa, jazz, and reggae. Musicians often play drums, *mejoranas*, bells, and flutes. Mejoranas are like guitars and have five strings. Panama's national dance is the *tamborito*. Its name means "little drum" in Spanish. Drums play as dancers show off speedy steps in a playful way.

TAMBORITO PERFORMANCE

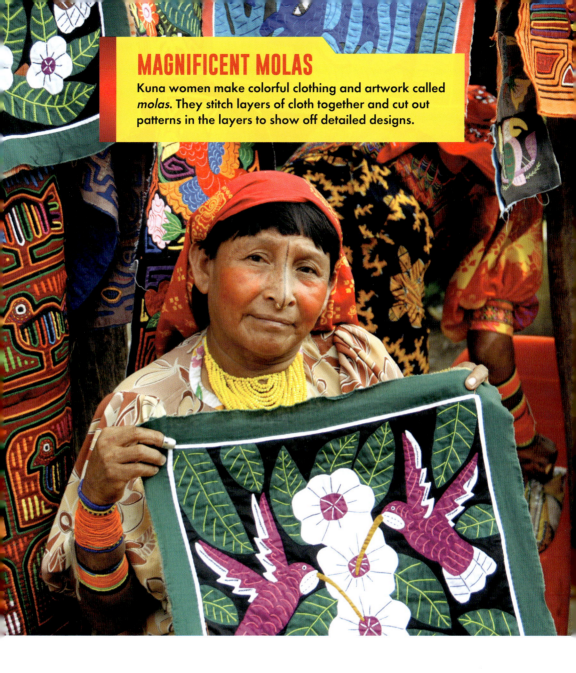

MAGNIFICENT MOLAS

Kuna women make colorful clothing and artwork called *molas*. They stitch layers of cloth together and cut out patterns in the layers to show off detailed designs.

Most Panamanians dress in styles similar to what people wear in the United States. People often wear **traditional** dress for special occasions. Women wear long **embroidered** outfits called *polleras*. Men wear a matching embroidered top with black pants.

17

Children in Panama must begin preschool at age 4. They attend primary school from ages 6 to 12. Classes include math, science, and language. Pre-secondary school lasts for three years. It is the last free and required stage of education. Secondary school students either get ready for college or train for jobs.

Over 6 out of 10 people in Panama have **service jobs**. Some work in banks or the **insurance** industry. Others have jobs in tourism, or they operate the Panama Canal. Panamanian workers build ships and make medicines. Farmers grow bananas, sugarcane, rice, and coffee.

COFFEE FARMER

BIG MONEY

In 2021, the Panama Canal earned $3.9 billion. Most of this money came from tolls that ships must pay to go through the canal.

PLAY

HIKING

Baseball is Panama's national sport. Fans cheer on their favorite professional teams. Many Panamanians play for fun, too. Soccer is also very popular throughout the country. People in Panama enjoy basketball and volleyball as well. Many people go hiking in their free time. In Panama City, people often hike through Metropolitan Natural Park.

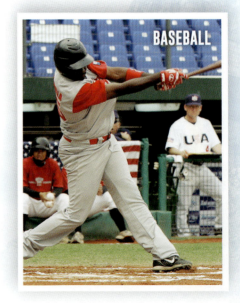

BASEBALL

In cities, Panamanians enjoy dancing at night clubs. People also listen to music or play cards with friends and family. Some take vacations by the beach or to the United States or Europe.

BEACH VACATION

MOLAS

Molas are a traditional Kuna artform. Common mola designs can include many shapes and animals, like turtles and cats. Create your mola from paper instead of fabric.

What You Need:

- black construction paper
- at least three other colors of construction paper
- pencil
- scissors
- glue

What You Do:

1. Look at some images of Kuna molas either online or in a book.

2. Draw a small shape or figure of your choosing onto one of the colored sheets of paper. Cut it out.

3. Place the cutout figure on top of a different colored sheet of paper. Lightly trace around the figure, but leave a 1/2-inch (1-centimeter) border around the shape's edges. Cut out the second figure.

4. Repeat steps 2 and 3 with several different colors of paper so you have at least a few figures that are the same shape but different sizes and colors.

5. Glue the biggest figure to the black construction paper. Continue gluing the smaller figures on top so that you can just see the layers underneath.

6. You can add some smaller paper cutout shapes in the corners or blank spaces of the black background sheet. Display your mola somewhere special!

A COOL TREAT

Raspados are snow cones flavored with fruit syrup. People in Panama often buy them from street carts. Popular flavors include lemon, strawberry, and grape. Some put condensed milk on top.

Most breakfasts in Panama start with coffee. People often eat eggs and fruit, including papayas and bananas. *Hojaldres*, a deep-fried bread dusted with powdered sugar, is also popular at breakfast. Coconut, rice, beans, and plantains are a part of many meals. *Sancocho* is a chicken stew made with yuca root and spices.

Ceviche is a popular seafood side. It has cubes of raw fish and onion soaked in lemon or lime juice. People often eat cornmeal pastries called *empanadas* as a snack. They are commonly filled with meat or cheese. *Tres leches* cake and flan are favorite desserts.

SANCOCHO

CEVICHE

CORN AND POTATO EMPANADAS

Have an adult help you make this easy dish for a snack or meal!

Ingredients:

1 large potato
1 package of pre-made pie crust
1 15-ounce can of corn, drained
1/2 cup shredded cheese
   (sharp cheddar or Mexican blend)
pinch of salt and pepper, to taste

Steps:

1. Peel the potato and cut it into 1/2-inch (1-centimeter) chunks. Put these into a small saucepan and cover with water. Boil until the potatoes are almost soft, about 13 to 17 minutes.

2. While the potatoes cook, roll out the pie crust according to the package directions. Use a large glass to cut out circles from the dough.

3. Drain the potatoes and place them into a large bowl. Add the corn. Add salt and pepper to the mixture and stir gently.

4. Place a tablespoon of the corn-potato filling onto each circle of dough. Sprinkle a little cheese on top.

5. Fold the pie crust over the filling. Use a fork to seal the edges.

6. Bake at 375 degrees Fahrenheit (191 degrees Celsius) for 8 to 10 minutes, or until golden brown. Let cool for a few minutes. Enjoy!

23

CARNIVAL

One of the most colorful events in Panama's year is Carnival. Celebrated in the days leading up to **Lent**, people dance, sing, and create amazing floats. Many Panamanians go on vacation over the Easter holiday. They often go to church and have a big meal with family on Easter Sunday.

November 28 marks when Panama gained independence from Spain. Fireworks and parades are part of the events. Big wreaths on doors and **Nativity** scenes in yards are common Christmas decorations. Many people go to midnight mass on Christmas. Panamanians celebrate their **culture** throughout the year!

INDEPENDENCE DAY CELEBRATION

A LIVELY GOODBYE

At midnight on New Year's Eve, Panamanians set life-sized dolls on fire. The dolls are stuffed with firecrackers. The loud noises they make are meant to say goodbye to bad things that happened the year before.

TIMELINE

1903
Panama becomes a fully independent country

1501
Rodrigo de Bastidas is the first European explorer to visit Panama

1966
Panama establishes its first national park, Parque Nacional Altos de Campana

1821
Panama gains independence from Spain and joins the union called Gran Colombia that includes Colombia, Venezuela, Ecuador, Panama, and parts of Brazil and Peru

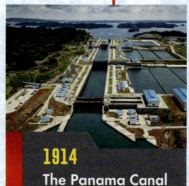

1914
The Panama Canal is completed

1999
Mireya Moscoso, Panama's first woman president, takes office

2005
Coiba National Park is named as a UNESCO World Heritage Site

1989
The United States invades Panama and drives out leader Manuel Noriega for criminal activity

1999
Panama gains control of the Panama Canal from the United States

Official Name: Republic of Panama

Flag of Panama: Four rectangles of the same size make up the flag of Panama. The top left rectangle is white with a blue star in the middle. The top right rectangle is solid red. The bottom left rectangle is solid blue. The bottom right rectangle is white with a red star in the center. The blue star stands for honesty and purity. The red star represents law and authority.

Area: 29,120 square miles
(75,420 square kilometers)

Capital City: Panama City

Important Cities: San Miguelito, Juan Diaz, David, Colón, Santiago

Population:
4,337,768 (2022 est.)

WHERE PEOPLE LIVE

COUNTRYSIDE
30.9%

CITY
69.1%

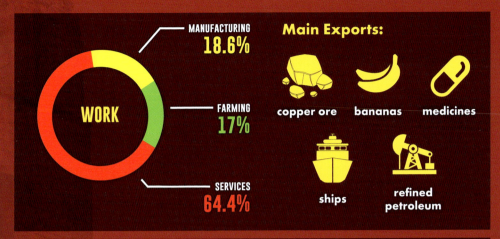

MANUFACTURING
18.6%

WORK

FARMING
17%

SERVICES
64.4%

Main Exports:

copper ore bananas medicines

ships refined petroleum

National Holiday:
Independence Day, November 3

Main Language:
Spanish (official)

Form of Government:
presidential republic

Title for Country Leader:
president (head of government and chief of state)

RELIGION

EVANGELICAL
30.2%

OTHER
8.9%

NONE
12.3%

ROMAN CATHOLIC
48.6%

Unit of Money:
Panamanian balboa and U.S. dollar

GLOSSARY

ancestors—relatives who lived a long time ago

bilingual—able to speak two languages

canal—a human-made waterway for boats

culture—the beliefs, arts, and ways of life in a place or society

embroidered—decorated with patterns sewn on with thread

immigrate—to move to a new country

indigenous—related to a group of people that began in the area

insurance—a business in which people pay money for protection against injuries or damages

isthmus—a narrow strip of land that connects two larger pieces of land; an isthmus lies between two bodies of water.

Lent—the period between Ash Wednesday and Easter when Christians often fast and express regret for their sins

Nativity—a scene or display that shows the birth of Jesus Christ

rain forest—a thick, green forest that receives a lot of rain

rural—related to the countryside

service jobs—jobs that perform tasks for people or businesses

snorkel—to swim using a tube to breathe underwater

tourists—people who travel to visit another place

traditional—related to customs, ideas, or beliefs handed down from one generation to the next

tropical—part of the tropics; the tropics is a hot, rainy region near the equator.

urban—related to cities and city life

volcano—a hole in the earth; when a volcano erupts, hot ash, gas, or melted rock called lava shoots out.

TO LEARN MORE

AT THE LIBRARY

Black, Vanessa. *Panama Canal*. Minneapolis, Minn.: Jump!, 2018.

Silva, Sadie. *Panama*. New York, N.Y.: Cavendish Square Publishing, 2022.

Spanier, Kristine. *Panama*. Minneapolis, Minn.: Jump!, 2022.

ON THE WEB

FACTSURFER

Factsurfer.com gives you a safe, fun way to find more information.

1. Go to www.factsurfer.com.

2. Enter "Panama" into the search box and click 🔍.

3. Select your book cover to see a list of related content.

INDEX

The images in this book are reproduced through the courtesy of: Diego Grandi/ Alamy, front cover; Image Professionals GmbH/ Alamy, pp. 4-5; Lara Bakalarova/ Alamy, p. 5 (Barú Volcano); akaramer, p. 5 (Biomuseo); UrbanUnique, p. 5 (Darién National Park); Solaarisys, p. 5 (Panama Canal); Prisma by Dukas Presseangentur GmbH/ Alamy, pp. 8, 20 (top); bgremler, p. 9 (top); Marianna Ianovska, p. 9 (bottom); buteo, p. 10 (toucan); Thorsten Spoerlein, p. 10 (agouti); Michael Smith ITWP, p. 10 (turtle); L-N, p. 10 (ocelot); worlswildlifewonders, pp. 10-11; GeorgePeters, p. 12; Francis Specker/ Alamy, p. 13 (top); hanohiki, p. 13 (bottom); Matyas Tehak, p. 14; Fotos593, p. 15; Cara Koch/ Alamy, p. 16; Danita Elimont/ Alamy, p. 17; Pictures Colour Library/ Alamy, p. 18; Joel Carillet, p. 19 (top); B. Franklin, p. 19 (bottom); Reuters/ Alamy, pp. 21 (top), 27 (left); agefotostock/ Alamy, p. 21 (top); oscar garces, p. 21 (bottom); Rob Crandall, p. 22; SteAck, p. 23 (top); BlueMoonStudioInc, p. 23 (middle); SGAPhoto, p. 23 (bottom); Melba Photo Agency/ Alamy, p. 24; Mark Pitt Images, p. 25; artemu kopylovk, p. 26; ian woolcock, p. 27 (right); Simon Belcher/ Alamy, p. 29 (banknote); Yaroslaff, p. 29 (coin).